Thank You, God

Written by J. Bradley Wigger

Illustrated by Jago

Eerdmans Books for Young Readers

Grand Rapids, Michigan • Cambridge, U.K.

To the young children of
Crescent Hill Presbyterian Church.
— J. B. W.

For my lovely wife Alex, and wonderful children, Lily and Rudy.
— J.

Text © 2014 J. Bradley Wigger
Illustrations © 2014 Jago

All rights reserved

Published in 2014 by Eerdmans Books for Young Readers,
an imprint of Wm. B. Eerdmans Publishing Co.
2140 Oak Industrial Dr. NE
Grand Rapids, Michigan 49505
P.O. Box 163, Cambridge CB3 9PU U.K.

www.eerdmans.com/youngreaders

Manufactured at Tien Wah Press
in Malaysia in July 2014, first printing

20 19 18 17 16 15 14   9 8 7 6 5 4 3 2 1

Library of Congress Cataloging-in-Publication Data

Wigger, J. Bradley.
Thank you, God / by J. Bradley Wigger; illustrated by Jago.
pages cm
ISBN 978-0-8028-5424-7
1. Gratitude — Prayers and devotions — Juvenile literature.
2. Christian children — Prayers and devotions. I. Jago, illustrator. II. Title.
BV4647.G8W53 2014
242'.62 — dc23
2013044346

The illustrations were rendered in digital paints and photographic textures.
The text type was set in ITC Tiepolo.

FSC
www.fsc.org
MIX
Paper from
responsible sources
FSC® C012700

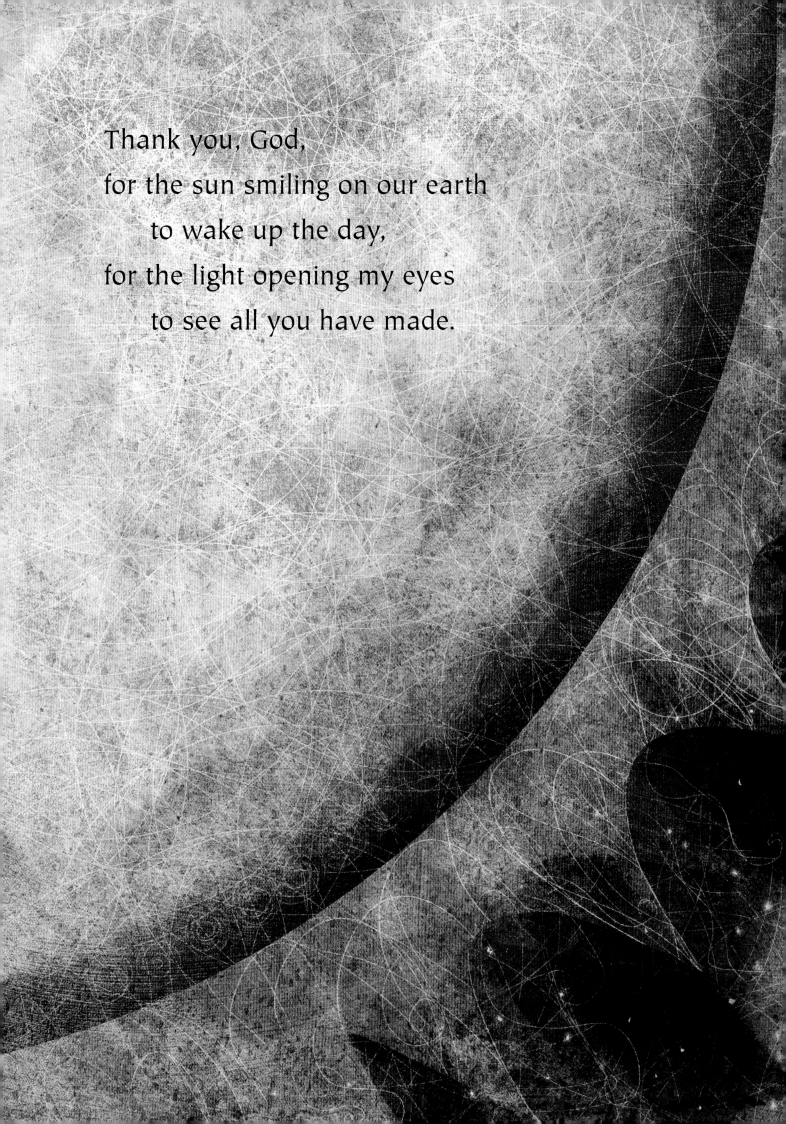

Thank you, God,
for the sun smiling on our earth
to wake up the day,
for the light opening my eyes
to see all you have made.

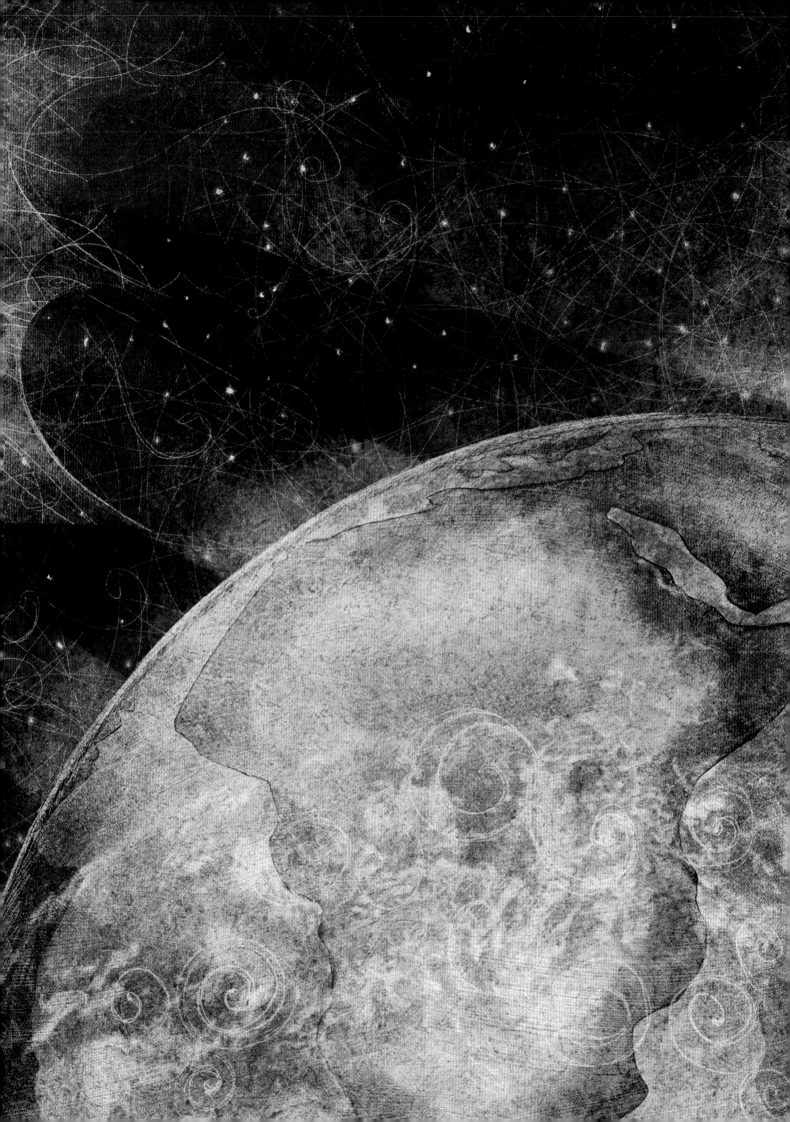

Thank you, God,
for family and friends,
  who hold and hug and care and kiss,
  who smile and laugh and play and love,
  who make my heart dance.

Thank you, God,
for home —
    the floor under my feet and ceiling over my head,
    with walls and windows around,
    keeping us close.

Thank you, God,
for meals together,
with good food to smell,
to taste,
and to fill my belly.

Thank you, God,
for the new words I learned today,
    for stories shared,
    for songs sung,
    and for love whispered.

Thank you, God,
for everything outside —
    trees and leaves and sky,
    dirt and flowers and fields,
    lakes and rivers and seas —
for making the world big and beautiful.

Thank you, God,
for the rain —
    drips, plops, and drops —

splashing the ground and pooling in puddles,
watering the land,
turning dirt into gardens.

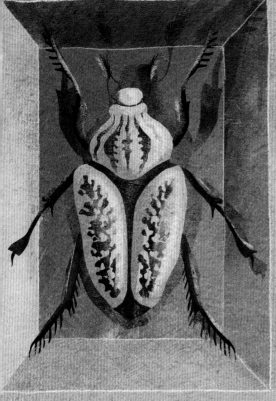

Thank you, God,
for all that breathes —
   bees and beetles
   and beluga whales,
   birds and baboons
   and bats in the breeze.

Thank you, God,
for the night,
  the stars and moon and planets far away,
  for calm and quiet
  and restful sleep,
  with dreams of a new day.

Bless you, God,
for this day,
for life,

for your love holding us together.
Amen.